IS BOOK BELONGS TO:

....

....

For Mum

A TEMPLAR BOOK

First published in the UK in 2019 by Templar Books,
an imprint of Templar Publishing, part of Bonnier Books UK,
The Plaza, 535 King's Road, London, SW10 0SZ
www.templarco.co.uk
www.bonnierbooks.co.uk

1 3 5 7 9 10 8 6 4 2

ISBN 978-1-7874-1-366-5

This book was typeset in Gill Sans and DK Frozen Memory
The illustrations were created with
mixed media and digital collage

Edited by Katie Haworth
Designed by Marty Cleary and Olivia Cook
Production Controller: Emma Kidd

Printed in Turkey

templar
books

WAKEY *BIRDS

MADDIE FROST

The jungle is an exotic place full of fascinating creatures. One of the most interesting species is called . . .

the Wakey Bird.

PEEP!

Wakey Birds get their name because
they have trouble falling asleep.
If we take a closer look, we can see why.

SIGH

They can't get
comfortable.

ACHOOOO!

GASP!

They are easily
spooked.

OOH!

They have
lots of
BIG
thoughts.

SCRITCH
SCRATCH

PEEP

They get itchy.

Thankfully, the jungle also has Soothing Shushers
and Go-To-Sleep Leapers.

A Soothing Shusher
looks like this . . .

SH-SH

and a Go-To-Sleep
Leaper looks like this!

GO TO SLEEP

These creatures help settle the Wakey Birds
down with calming noises.

Except for the
Littlest Wakey Bird.

PEEP!

Then the birds go back to their nests where they finally close their eyes and drift off to sleep.

Tonight,

she is

just

not

tired.

PEEP

It's not much fun being the only one awake.

Instead of sleeping, she wants to play a game
of hide-and-go-peep. Except there are no other
Wakeys to come and find her.

She's getting lonely.   She's getting very sad.   She's getting . . .

a **STICK**

to wake the others up!

BANG!

BANG!

BANG!

BANG!

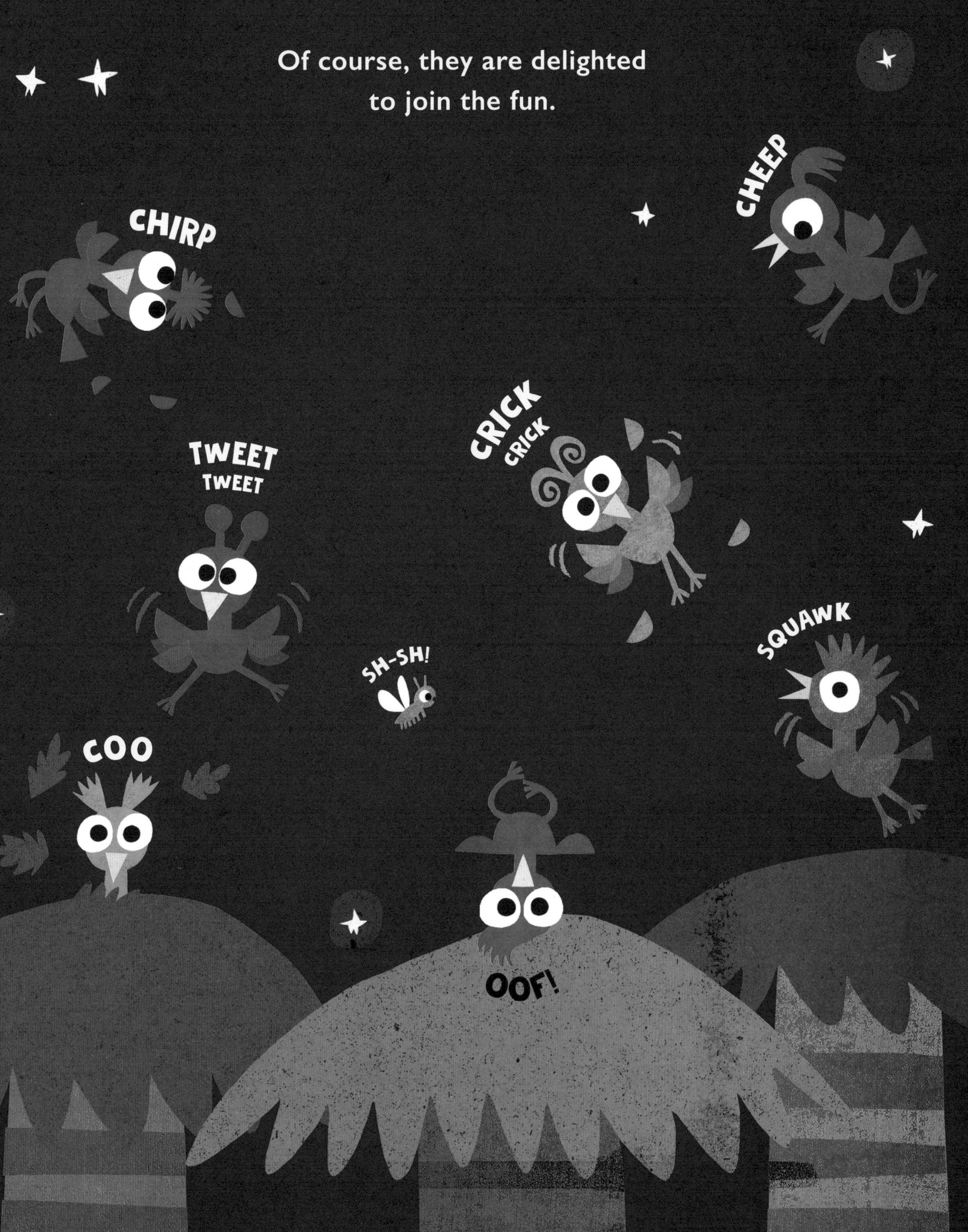

Of course, they are delighted
to join the fun.

But now things have got **very loud!**
These Wakeys need to watch out . . .

or they'll wake up
the loudest animal
in the jungle.

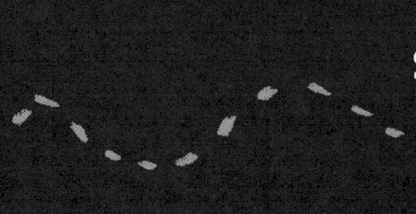

The Shrieking Monkey.

SSShHHHH
RRRRIIIII
IIEEEEEE
EEKKKKK
IIIIIIIII

No! No! No! It is definitely way too **loud** and this time they really need to be careful . . .

BANG
BANG
BANG

or they will disturb the one animal
that should never, **ever** be disturbed.

The Dreaded Jungle Beast.

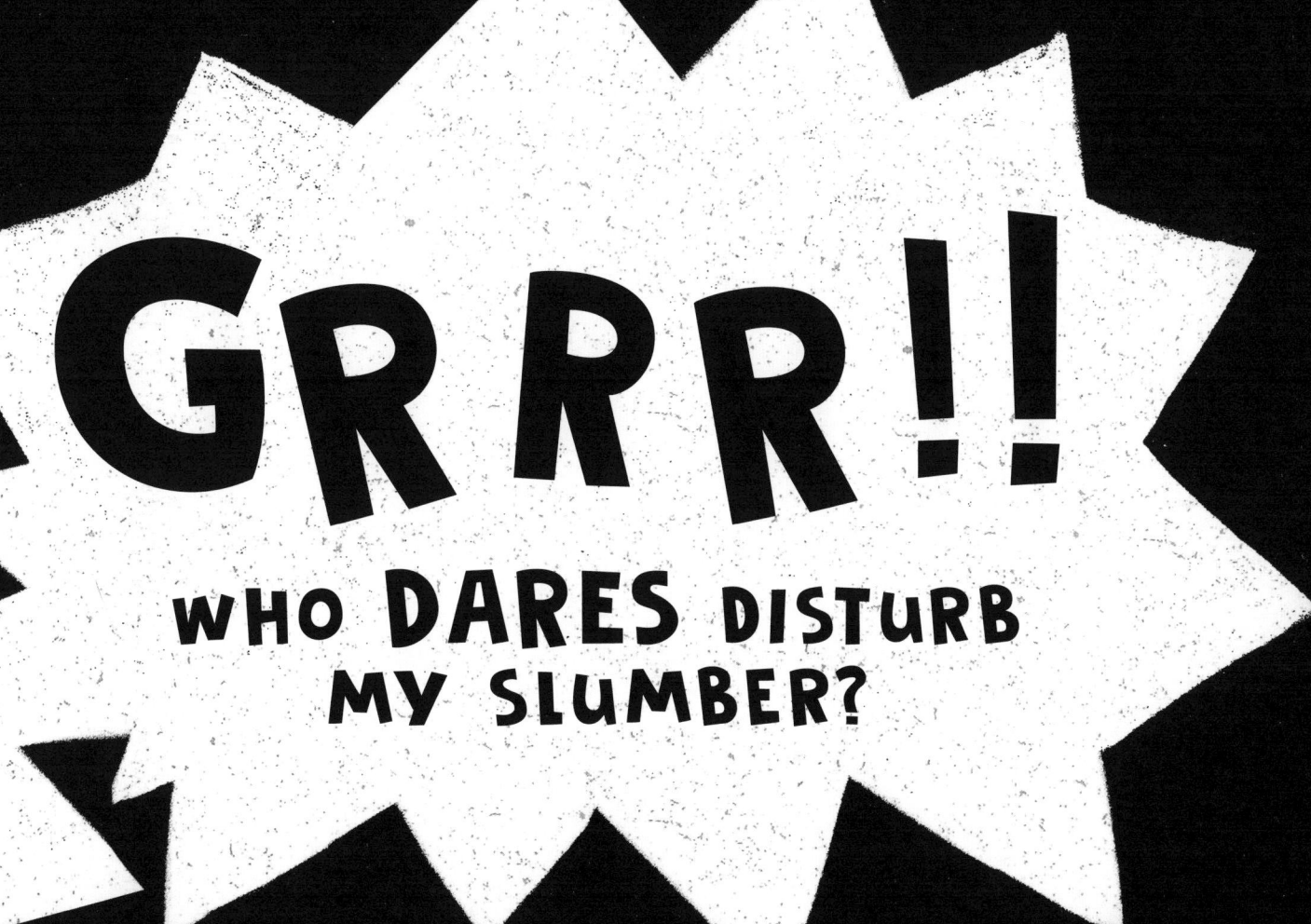

Oh dear.

The Dreaded Jungle Beast has come out of his cave.

The Littlest Wakey Bird is so scared she can't move. She had better speak up before she gets **chomped!**

PEEP, PEEP
I CAN'T SLEEP.

The Dreaded Jungle Beast goes
back into his deep, dark cave.
What is he doing?

The Littlest Wakey Bird is scared she'll
become a midnight snack.

She is trembling with terror!

Finally the Beast returns with a

STOMP, STOMP, STOMP.

He's carrying a **great big . . .**

. . . storybook!

The Wakey Birds have never heard a story before.
They huddle in nice and close . . .

and the Dreaded Jungle Beast begins
to read in his deep, beastly voice.

Soon the Wakey Birds
aren't feeling so wakey
anymore.

But the Littlest
Wakey Bird is **still**
not asleep.

PEEP!

Never mind. She is now.

And the rest of the jungle is too.